PUBLIC SEX TALES

EXPLICIT DIRTY EROTICA SHORT STORIES

CHARA GLADEY

plicit Press

CHAPTER 1

ON THE HORIZON

THE SAND WAS STILL warm beneath her feet, the air coming in off the bright blue sea-salty and cool. Nineteen-year-old Skye Adams could smell the rainy season just a few days away. Her all-female crew would head into one of the towns they usually frequented to wait out the week of storms. No one on the *Black Waters* was scared to sail in any weather, but Skye saw no point roaming the seas if their marks were safely hidden away. Although, she had to admit, by the time the rains ended, she was desperate to be back on her ship, hunting the high seas for whatever treasure she could find.

She tossed back her curls, the brilliant bittersweet red shimmering in the late afternoon sun, and squinted her aquamarine eyes, gaze locked on the figure strolling up the beach. She didn't need to see his features to recognize the captain of the *Golden Waters*. Wind-swept copper hair that could use a trim, serious blue-gray eye, a ruggedly hand-some face, tanned from hours aboard his own ship, and a tall, muscular body that Skye knew as well as her own. She'd mapped every scar, could trace them in her sleep;

every new one made her heart clench. Not that she'd ever tell him that. She and Brady had been lovers for a couple years now and enjoyed their time together, but she had no illusions about life together. After all, there was no such thing as two captains on a ship.

Neither one spoke as they drew closer to each other. Their eyes locked as they crossed the beach and they didn't need words to know what the other was thinking. Brady reached for her first, fingers deftly relieving Skye of her clothes even as her hands moved to do the same for him. Their mouths met even as the ocean breeze caressed each newly bared inch and Skye made a noise in the back of her throat. Brady chuckled as he parted her lips, thrusting his tongue into her mouth. Skye pushed against his chest and he grabbed her arms, tumbling them both to the ground.

They rolled across the sand, tongues dueling for dominance even as they fought for control.

Brady buried his hand in Skye's thick curls, cupping the back of her skull as he deepened their kiss. His free hand traveled the length of her athletic body, over her back down to the swell of her ass, and back up again, unconsciously tracing the lines of her various scars. She wasn't quite so gentle, nails raking the full length of his back and over his muscular ass, each pass drawing a gasp from his lips and a twitch from the hard length pressed against her hip.

Brady dropped his hand from Skye's head, breaking their kiss to gasp for air. His eyes met hers, seeking permission as he reached between them. Skye parted her legs, back arching as Brady's index finger slipped between her folds. He smiled as she whimpered, pushing her hips forward, trying to get more friction where she needed it the most.

When the tip of his finger teased around the edges, Skye growled, hands pushing at Brady's shoulders.

"I'm wet, just fuck me already," Skye was the first to break the relative silence.

He pushed his finger inside her tight channel and Skye made a strangled sound that may have been one of encouragement or may have been a string of vulgarities. She scowled but pressed down, forcing his finger deeper even as she maneuvered her hand to wrap her fingers around his hard cock. Brady sucked in air as she began to move her hand, the grains of sand on her palm creating near-painful friction against his sensitive skin.

"I said," she punctuated each word with alternating squeezes and strokes. "I'm wet. Fuck me."

Brady withdrew his finger and grabbed Skye's leg, hooking it around his waist. He needed very little assistance for his cock to find her entrance and her fingers dug into his hip as he buried himself inside her with one quick movement.

"Fuck," Skye cried out as he filled her. The initial penetration was always like this. Her juices allowed him to slide in with just the right amount of friction. Her walls clung to his steel length as he sheathed himself in her tight heat. The nearly-to-full sensation of being stretched around him. The sense of completion as their bodies came together.

Brady rocked his hips, letting himself slip in and out just enough to help Skye adjust, and then rolled them over so that Skye was on her back. He raised himself on his arms so that just their lower bodies were touching, her ankles crossing just below his ass. He held himself there for a moment, staring down at her with a burning gaze.

Skye lifted her hips, urging him to move. Her fingers ran over the muscles in his arms as Brady started to thrust, nearly withdrawing before snapping forward again, each one making Skye swear as his cock ran over that spot inside her that sent sparks of pleasure through her body. He went deeper and faster, forcing the air from her lungs.

The familiar tightening heat in her lower belly told her that she was close and Skye moved her hands to her breasts. Her fingers tugged at her nipples, sending jolts of pleasure straight to her pussy as the caramel-colored flesh hardened. She raised her hips to meet Brady; pushing her towards release and tightening her muscles each time he pulled back, wanting him to join her.

It was the ocean that did them in. The first cool wave that broke across their over-heated flesh shocked them both and pushed them over the edge. Brady covered her mouth with his, swallowing her cries as his body shuddered against hers. It was fitting, Skye thought, and that they'd found their pleasure in the water they both loved so much. They lay there for a few minutes, catching their breath and letting the sea wash over them. When Brady rolled off of her, Skye up.

"We'll be riding the coast after the storms stop," Brady got to his feet. "Aye," Skye agreed. "And we'll dock at Morristown to trade after our haul."

"Perhaps I will see you there," Brady laced up his breeches and picked up his shirt. Skye nodded, pulling her shirt over her head.

"Until then," he held her gaze for a brief moment before

turning and walking back up the beach to where his ship waited.

Skye watched him go as she finished dressing. She grimaced as she ran a hand through her curls. The next time they fucked on a beach, she was going to be on top.

CHAPTER 2

THE DARK HOUSE

EIGHTEEN-YEAR-OLD CICI ROSE stared up at the dilapidated mansion. Her blue-green eyes were narrowed in concentration as they searched for signs of paranormal activity. She ran a hand through her short white-blond hair and glanced at her twenty-year-old boyfriend. Davis Forester raised an eyebrow, the question clear in his dark gray eyes, but he asked it anyway.

"Think there's anything to the stories?"

"You need a haircut," Cici didn't answer his question as she glanced around. No one else could be seen. She grabbed Davis's hand and pulled him after her.

"You're going to cut my hair here? Now?" Davis shook his dark brown hair out of his eyes and he let her drag him onto the porch. He didn't bother pointing out her abrupt change in direction.

"It's nearly midnight and the 'haunted house' we drove fourteen hours to see is just an old wreck," Cici yanked Davis to her, pressing her curves against his lean body.

"There's no evidence that a Woman in White is here. If I can't hunt, I want to fuck."

Davis grinned. He wrapped his arms around her, grinding his hips against hers. It never took him long to get in the mood. They would've been suited for each other even if they hadn't been brought together by the tragedies of their respective pasts. For instance, both had insanely high sex drives and a certain predilection for public places.

He bent his head and captured her lips, mouth bruising against hers as he forced his tongue into her mouth. She could taste the cinnamon gum he'd been chewing for the past hour. He slid his hands under her t-shirt, his touch blazing across her skin.

Cici groaned into her boyfriend's mouth, fingers scrabbling at his waist, unzipping his pants. She worked her hand inside, reveling in the sound he made when her hand curled around the hard length she knew so well. She jerked him roughly and he bit her bottom lip in retaliation, sending a jolt straight to her pussy. He spun them around until they were up against one crumbling porch wall. Only then did he break their kiss.

"What are you in the mood for?" Davis nuzzled just under her ear. His hands skimmed up over her ribcage, thumbs brushing against the undersides of her full breasts. "Fingers?" He pinched her nipples through two layers of material. "Or cock?" He circled behind her and slipped his hand into the waistband of her jeans, fingers tracing the elastic of her panties. "Do you want me in your ass or pussy?"

"Surprise me," Cici breathed, pushing her ass back against Davis, eliciting a hiss.

. . .

"You've got it," Davis growled. He bent Cici towards the porch wall, fingers roughly yanking at her shorts. He tugged down the garment as Cici placed her palms flat on the top of the wall, ignoring the damp moss and the awkward angle at which she was now bent.

She shivered as her skin was exposed to the cool night air. A gentle breeze caressed her overheated skin and she shifted her weight.

"Spread your legs," Davis ordered, kicking her ankles apart when she didn't move fast enough. "Look at you," he ran a finger between her folds and she whimpered. "Wet and ready for me." He shoved his finger into her cunt. Cici yelped. "And so tight."

"Please," Cici pleaded. Her nipples were hot bullet points, straining against her bra and t-shirt, and her pussy throbbed with need.

Davis took hold of her hips and buried himself inside his girlfriend with a thrust forceful enough to make her squeal. He didn't give her any time to adjust, to think. One hand reached around and pressed a finger against her lips.

"Suck," Davis's breathing was ragged.

Cici opened her mouth, letting Davis's finger slip inside. Her tongue circled the digit, tasting the sale from his flesh.

"That's right, get it nice and wet," Davis was breathless but continued to talk. "I'm going to put it in your ass and you're going to cum."

Cici's body shuddered, Davis's words having the desired effect. Her body hummed with energy, the illicit nature of their actions heightening the experience. When Davis slid his finger from her mouth, she began to moan, the familiar pressure building in her belly. She wriggled as she felt the gentle touch of his fingertip against the puckered flesh of her asshole.

"So greedy," Davis chuckled, the vibration going straight through her. Without warning, he shoved his finger into her ass and Cici screamed, body going rigid as she came.

"That's my girl," Davis panted as he slammed into her, forcing his cock past the spasming muscles. When Cici's knees buckled, he held her with one arm, refusing to stop his finger from fucking her ass while he pounded into her. His muscles protested but he ignored the burning, determined to make her climax one more time.

"I'm going to cum inside you; make you wear just your jeans while we go to a hotel. I want you walking in, worried that everyone will see a damp spot and know it's my cum leaking out of your pussy."

Cici made an inarticulate noise. She was going to explode. She knew it. The pleasure was coursing through her veins, flames of near agony-ecstasy as she sped towards the cliff. She wouldn't survive Davis's assault, his cock driving her forward so that she had to dig her nails into the moss. She was crying out now, the night echoing back the sound.

"Ci," Davis called out her name as he buried himself balls deep, spilling deep inside her.

The sensation of her boyfriend's warmth spurting into her cunt was all she needed to come apart. She made no sound this time, couldn't make a sound, as the world grayed out.

When she came to, Davis had her cradled in his lap, his heartbeat thrumming against her back.

. . .

His lips were against her ear, murmuring sweet nothings as his fingers stroked her skin. After a moment, she spoke. "Hotel?"

"Good idea," Davis agreed. "We need to decide where to go next."

"Maybe this time we can actually start working tomorrow rather than two days from now," Cici grinned.

"Maybe," Davis returned the smile. "But I doubt it."

CHAPTER 3

IRRESISTIBLE

THE LIGHTS HADN'T EVEN DIMMED before twenty-two-year-old Davis Bannerman was sliding his hand under his girlfriend's sweater. Twenty-two-year-old Kassidy Dewan glared at him, the expression in her cyan eyes more turned on than angry. She tossed her walnut brown curls over her shoulder, grabbed his wrist, and hissed, "What do you think you're doing?"

Davis leaned closer, pitching his voice low so that only she could hear it. His dark chocolate eyes were nearly black with desire. "I'm feeling you up, what do you think I'm doing?" He moved his hand higher, skimming across the bare expanse of her stomach up to her bra. His palm burned through the cotton as he cupped her breast and Kassidy shifted in her seat.

"Stop that," she protested but made no attempt to pull his hand away.

"I know you, Kass," Davis put his other arm around her shoulders as the previews began to roll. "You act like you don't want this, that you want me to stop, but I know the truth. I can feel your nipple hardening under my palm and I'll bet your panties are getting wet just thinking about what I might do next."

Kassidy bit back a groan and pressed her thighs together. He was right. The idea that anyone around them could see them spoke to something deep inside that she never talked about, something that Davis had sensed from the moment they'd started dating four months ago. She'd been attracted to him instantly. With his short black hair, silky cocoa-colored skin and lean body, every girl in the club had been staring but she was the one he'd singled out.

"Pick up my coat," Davis instructed.

Kassidy reached for it, hands trembling as she pulled it over herself, a thrill of anticipation running through her. She didn't have to wait long. As soon as she was covered, Davis's nimble fingers worked open the front clasp of her bra, freeing her B-cups. Instantly, she knew that he'd been planning this from the moment he'd said they should go to a movie. He'd specifically requested a relatively loose pair of pants and sweater, as well as her pale green bra and panties. Kassidy had assumed it was for something at the end of the night, a quick fuck in his car, perhaps. This hadn't crossed her mind.

"I can picture these in my mind," Davis put his lips against her ear. His hand ran over her smooth skin, fingers greedy as they kneaded her firm flesh. "Creamy skin with just fading tan lines." He traced his finger along where he knew the line ran across her skin. "Nipples the color of peaches." When his finger and thumb closed around her nipple, Kassidy made a noise that she quickly turned into a cough.

"Shh," Davis flicked out his tongue, running it along the outside of her ear. "We wouldn't want someone to call an usher." He sucked her earlobe into his mouth as he dropped his hand down to the waist of her pants.

Kassidy sucked in a breath as his fingers snapped the button, her entire body tensing. "Open your legs for me," he nipped at her earlobe. "And remember to stay quiet."

She parted her legs and shoved the side of her hand into her mouth. Two seconds later, she was glad she had. Davis's fingers slipped between her folds, rubbing her clit on their way to her now- throbbing pussy. When he slid two fingers inside, her body jerked and her teeth clamped down on her hand.

"You're so hot and tight around my fingers, baby," Davis whispered. "Every time I move my hand, your walls grip me, like they don't ever want me to leave. Is that true? Do you want my hand between your legs forever?" He pressed his palm against her clit and she writhed. "Or is there something else you'd like more?"

Kassidy's eyes were wide as she looked at him. Her body was already shaking, unable to process so much at once. The forbidden nature of what they were doing. The scratchy wool of her sweater against her sensitized nipples. The fingers in her cunt. The pressure on her clit.

"Don't worry, we're not going to fuck," he chuckled, the sound going straight to her pussy. "We need to save something for next time." She whimpered.

"Touch your tits," Davis curled his fingers and Kassidy yelped, thankful that her hand muffled the sound. "Come on, tug on those nipples."

Her fingers were closing around one little hard pebble before she realized what she was doing.

She rolled the crinkled flesh and a jolt shot through her.

"And now you're going to cum," he crooked his fingers again and Kassidy's body convulsed, hips bucking up as her orgasm rocked her.

His fingers were out and up at her mouth before she'd started coming down. She opened her mouth instinctively, sucking her juices from his fingers even as her muscles twitched with aftershocks.

"That's a good girl," Davis picked up the hand Kassidy's had in her mouth. He pressed his lips against the teeth marks she'd left in her flesh. "Now," he pressed their joined hands against his crotch. "Your turn."

Kassidy cupped him through his pants and he gave a low groan that made her cunt throb. She slipped her hand under his waistband, eyebrows shooting up in surprise as she realized he hadn't worn his usual boxers. Her hand closed around his hard length, fingers barely able to wrap around the thick shaft. She watched him as she began to move her hand. She knew exactly what he liked, how to twist her wrist at the top with every other stroke, how to brush her thumb across his slit, and she loved watching his face as she did it. Desire coiled low in her belly as she watched pleasure play across his features. He moaned.

"Shh," she echoed his earlier statement. "We don't want someone calling an usher."

Mimicking her, Davis stuffed his fist into his mouth. It came not a second too soon. Kassidy squeezed with just the right amount of pressure and Davis's cock pulsed in her hand. His cum spilled over her hand as she continued to run her hand over his softening flesh until she felt his hips pull back. Only then did she release him.

Their eyes locked as she removed her hand from his pants and raised it to his mouth. Without breaking their gaze, he took her fingers into his mouth, cleaning himself from her flesh. When her hand dropped into her lap, he leaned forward and covered her mouth with his. His tongue parted her lips and she tasted him on her tongue, his essence mingling with her own. He pulled back, his lips touching hers as he whispered. "I need to go to the restroom to clean up. Feel free to join me." His eyes flicked to the screen, then back to her face. "I really didn't want to see this movie anyway."

Kassidy watched him go. She waited only as long as it took to fix her clothes before following.

She didn't want to watch the movie either.

CHAPTER 4

FIRST DATE CONCERT FUCK

THE MADONNA CONCERT ROCKED. I always wanted to go; so when Foxy, my next-door neighbor said, "I've got an extra ticket do you want to go?" I agreed right away. Foxy was eighteen years old and she loved sex. Somehow, I wasn't her type. We were like two ships coming into port bogged down in our own private lives. Foxy said she'd pick me up at eight o'clock for the evening concert.

I showered, put on my Madonna Truth or Dare T-shirt, and ran down my apartment stairs. Foxy waited in her blue Audi sports car. I hopped in the passenger seat and she pulled from the curb like we were auditioning for the Indy 500. I didn't want to slow her down. We might as well get a good seat and maybe even an autograph from Madonna backstage if possible.

Crowded doesn't even begin to describe the venue. We got to our seats and I must admit being surrounded by screaming yelling gorgeous Madonna fans rocked. Foxy noticed my wandering eye and she took my hand and said, "This is our first date."

"Really?" She surprised me and being approached by

someone, well as foxy, as Foxy made my day. The concert went on and we smiled a lot. Then on impulse, Foxy suddenly kissed me on the cheek.

I turned around and took her face in my hands and French kissed her. We stood there in the stands grinding and sucking one another's faces when Foxy said, "I have to go to the ladies' room."

I expected her to go and come back. To my surprise, she held onto my hand while leaving the aisle! We made our way up the long stadium stairs and out to the concession stands. Foxy pulled me towards the ladies' room, right when I started to depart to the men's room. "No one will be here now!" she cooed. "If we wait until the song break, I'll never get to piss."

Inside the ladies' room, Foxy wasn't the only one preplanning the song break. Two other girls, both about Foxy's age, one wearing a spiked blue hairstyle and several nose rings laughed at us holding hands. Her friend, a blonde, in tight light blue stretch pants and a distressed black Madonna tour T-shirt just smiled.

Foxy took me into the stall and she raised her black-mini skirt over her hips. She squatted, tinkled, and never took her eyes off me. Finally, the two girls stopped giggling and left the bathroom. Foxy rolled off some tissue paper and wiped herself. She flushed the toilet and turned around. "Fuck me!"

On impulse, I started to balk. I'd never been caught in the women's bathroom before. I didn't know if it was a crime or not. Then as she leaned over the toilet, her own Truth or Dare shirt holding up her mini skirt, I couldn't resist going down on her pussy.

"Fuck me! Don't lick me!" Foxy hissed. "I know you've

been dying to get into my hot wet and wetter snatch all summer.

"You know your men, Foxy." I licked her pussy slit from her clit to her fuck hole one last time and unbuckled my pants. "This is the most amazing first date ever!"

I spoke too soon. Millions of footsteps started rushing and crowding into the bathroom. I noticed as I looked down at my pants around my ankles several different girls' heads flashing past the stall door's bottom looking for empty stalls. They laughed and said, "Some guy is fucking his girlfriend in stall three."

Foxy didn't say anything. I realized her kink related to exhibitionism. She knew we'd be fucking when several women and girls would be using the bathroom. I didn't care. I rubbed my hands all over Foxy's long slim, tanned thighs. She wore her thick black hair in a five-hair-strand braid. I'm a sucker for braided hair. I'm a sucker for doggy style. Foxy leaned her head down facing the stall wall over the toilet. She reached back shyly and her hand grazed my dick meat. She tested its fullness. She then bumped her rump back drawing my attention away from her pretty black strands of hair on her neck to her hot steamy crotch.

Foxy's work-of-art pussy contours needed to be in a museum instead of between her legs. Her long narrow clit curved under and almost down to her pee hole. She had this long distance from her pee hole to her fuck slot. Her barely-there inner labia never reached beyond her outer labia lips. I pushed my bloated cock up against her groin. Foxy moaned. All the women in the bathroom moaned in mock or in desired admiration. I did not know. I put the length of my growing, straining cock meat under her pelvic floor. I tapped my penis under her, hitting her clit, labia lips, and fuck hole at the same time.

"Fuck her!" I heard a high-pitched squeal voice yell.

I raised my head to see two girls, standing on the toilet in the next stall watching us. I positioned my steel desire and pushed it inside Foxy's wet box. Both women sighed and took more cell phone pictures. I hoped this wasn't going on the Internet. My face would be visible. Foxy kept her face lowered so she was anonymous.

My cave hunter reached up higher and higher into Foxy's squishy, wet-sounding fuck slice. I thrust hard in and out. Foxy rocked back on her heels seducing my cock and balls to release their boiling cum. I held back.

Foxy reached back and grabbed my balls forcing me to stay inside her. My hips bucked and holding back became impossible. So with the growing audience above the stalls watching us fuck, I pummeled my hips into the soft pinkness of Foxy's cunt repeatedly, until at last, Foxy screamed. I growled.

The girls sighed and all in the bathroom clapped. Foxy grabbed more toilet paper and wiped the excess of sperm leaking from her boiling hot cunt. She lowered her miniskirt and raised my pants. We left out of there without washing our hands as if we owned that bathroom and went back to the concert.

Foxy and I repeated the kinky act at the next concert to an even bigger crowd. What I learned is that exhibitionist first dates are just as exciting as the second and third times. People love to watch a public fuck, more than the concerts itself.

CHAPTER 5

ISLAND ADVENTURES – AN EXPERIENCE

HER VACATION WAS MEANT to be a romantic getaway for her and her husband Steve, but now, with Steve gone almost every day, Amarie had now found a new love interest. Daniel was handsome and, more importantly, he was witty and adventurous. He had promised to show her the time of her life on the island. As they made their way to the beach, he stopped in a secluded area and complimented her beauty.

"Amarie...your body is so wonderful. I'd love to spend one day just kissing you and another just touching you, everywhere." He pulled her into his arms, lowering her to the blanket, offering him no resistance.

She lay on her back, Daniel beside her. He continued kissing her, one hand cupping her breast, gently but firmly massaging it with his hand. Amarie moaned deeply at his touch, arching her back so her breast filled his hand. He broke away from her kiss, looking down at her, pulling the top of her bikini aside and exposing one breast. He licked his fingers and then rubbed them over her nipple, watching as it grew hard beneath his wet fingers.

Amarie watched, mesmerized by Daniel's attention to her breast, as he bent his head and licked the now-hardened nipple, his tongue flicking back and forth, sending shivers through her body. She was so used to Paul's rough foreplay that she was momentarily startled by how arousing something so gently could be.

Daniel continued playing with her breast, kissing and licking the skin, nipping gently with his teeth, occasionally sucking the nipple slowly. She could feel his erection against her hip and she tried to reach down to touch him. He shook his head against her breast.

"No, love. Just lay back and let me love you for a little bit." Amarie was completely unprepared to hear that. She closed her eyes; letting the sun make patterns on her eyelids as she let the sensations of Daniel's mouth on her breast create a slow burn deep in her. Daniel had freed her other breast, now paying lavish attention to it, licking and kissing, gently blowing on her wet skin. That simple act made her gasp, sending a wave of goosebumps across her skin.

With gentle hands, Daniel began working Amarie's bikini bottom down over her hips. She raised herself up slightly, allowing him to slide the garment down her legs and over her feet. He trailed a line of kisses down her stomach, licking her navel, dipping his tongue into it, nibbling the edge.

With warm hands, he gently spread Amarie's legs, sliding his hands beneath her ass, lifting her pussy toward his mouth as he bent his head to her, his tongue slowly tracing along the edge of her slit. She could feel every motion his tongue made, every cell of her body focused on the heat between her legs. Daniel parted her slit with his fingers, exposing her clit to his kiss. As he gently licked her clit, circling it with his tongue, Amarie tensed, waiting for the familiar and somewhat overwhelming feeling Paul's tongue on her clit caused, and her usually an abrupt and intense reaction. But with Daniel, it was different; it was amazing in its own way, gentle and sweet, and very erotic. His tongue began moving faster, working over her clit and sliding into her pussy.

She could feel herself growing wetter by the minute.

Amarie began rocking her hips back and forth in time to Daniel's probing tongue. Her body was building to an orgasm and she knew it was going to be intense. But she also wanted to feel what Daniel had done to her the night before. She reached down, cupping his face in her hands.

"Daniel..." She sat up, looking at him. She wasn't quite sure how to ask for this. "Wait...can you....last night, you did...something..." her voice trailed off. Daniel smiled up at her.

"Do you mean what I did to you on the beach, with my fingers?" Amarie nodded. "For you, I'd do anything. All you need do is ask." Daniel adjusted his position between Amarie's legs, sliding two fingers into her pussy. Amarie moaned in anticipation, thrusting her hips up to meet his fingers.

"Just relax, love. Let me do the work." Daniel began slowly moving his fingers, working them around inside Amarie's pussy. They both knew when he found the spot; she let out a sharp cry as her body jerked uncontrollably beneath Daniel's touch, fluid squirting from her pussy. She lay back on the blanket, closing her eyes. She was still mildly embarrassed by the thought of uncontrollably squirting liquid from her pussy.

"Ah, we have found that special spot, love." Daniel began fingering Amarie as her body continued moving on its own. She could feel liquid trickling between her ass cheeks and then, to her shock, she felt Daniel's lips and tongue back at her pussy. He began working his fingers faster, making her body convulse, Daniel licking her juices as they ran from her body. She tried feebly to push his head away from her pussy. He lifted his head briefly.

"You taste better than the finest wine, Amarie. Don't be embarrassed by how your body reacts; it's normal. You're a very sensual woman. Just relax and let go...let your body respond."

He bent his head again, his fingers still hitting the sweet spot, her body still convulsing and twitching. Daniel's tongue was swirling around her clit, making her body sing with arousal. She could feel her orgasm building, feel herself losing control.

Daniel sent her over the edge by pulling her clit into his mouth, sucking on it. Between his fingers and mouth, the sensations became overwhelming for Amarie. Her orgasm broke then, her hips bucking up against Daniel's face, back arching off the blanket. She twisted from side to side, bracing herself against the ground with her arms. She cried out over and over, her body dissolving into one long continuous quivering mass. Daniel had removed his fingers from her, but kept his mouth against her pussy, moaning against her, licking the juices that ran from her.

When she finally came back to reality, her orgasm fading and her body stilling, she looked down at Daniel. He was holding her hips, his cheek resting on her thigh, looking up at her, smiling.

"And is that what you were looking for, love? Because if it's something else you want, I'll do that too."

"No, that was it. Thank you. It was pretty amazing." She sat up. "Very amazing. How did you learn to do that?"

"Ah, but I cannot give away my secrets." Daniel sat up.

Amarie noticed his huge erection tenting the front of his swim trunks. She felt guilty. Daniel was watching her, following her gaze to his massive erection.

"Amarie, I want to make love to you, but not here. I want to take you to a special place. Come with me." He stood holding out his hand. She stood, adjusting her bikini top and pulling her bottom back on.

Amarie realized they were going behind the falling water. Daniel held her hand and guided her over several large rocks until they were in a space behind the waterfall, the water making a moving curtain across the front, hiding them from view. They stood on a strip of rocky sand that ran around the edge of the space with smaller streams of water falling inside the space; the cool water trickling over her heated skin felt wonderful.

"This is beautiful, Daniel. It's a magical place." She turned to him as he pulled her into his arms.

"Yes, love, it is." He bent his head, capturing her mouth with his. Amarie felt his hard cock poking her; she reached down to hold him but Daniel backed away.

"One touch and I'd explode." He laughed. "I'm fairly well heated at the moment. I want to make love to you now, Amarie, in the worst way." His voice had grown husky, and his eyes are hooded and dark. "Let me make love to you, let me feel you around my cock. I want to be inside of you." Amarie nodded.

With one graceful movement, Daniel stripped off his swim trunks. Amarie worked her bikini bottom down over her hips, dropping it on the sand. Daniel stood naked in front of her, gloriously naked, his massive cock sticking out in front of him, waiting for her.

"Oh, God, Amarie. You're so gorgeous." He pulled her to him briefly, and then turned her around, his cock rubbing against her ass. "It's not comfortable on the ground; is this alright? From behind? You can brace yourself on the rocks. I'll hold you so you don't topple over." Amarie nodded.

She could feel Daniel moving behind her and then she felt the head of his cock rubbing against her pussy. He held still a moment and then slowly slid himself into her pussy, groaning loudly as he entered her. He was hot and hard and began moving inside her quickly. Amarie sensed he really was close to exploding.

Daniel sped up his movements, his hips curving forward, knees bent as he thrust into her. Amarie held onto the rock in front of her, looking over her shoulder at Daniel. His head was tipped back, his mouth open, a look of pure bliss on his face. She listened as his breathing became ragged, his moans getting louder. His thrusts became faster, harder and suddenly he came inside her, shouting out as his orgasm broke. He pushed hard into her once and then held himself still as his cock pumped his come into her.

He held himself inside her for a minute after his orgasm faded. He pulled himself out of her, helping her stand and pulling her into his arms.

"That was amazing, Amarie." He ran a finger down her nose, kissing her on the mouth. "You're amazing, Amarie." He slapped her lightly on her ass. She yelped in surprise.

ABOUT THE AUTHOR

Chara Gladey is an emerging erotica author of many erotica kinks and sub-genres. Be sure to check out other books and leave a review if this story got you hot!

Visit my blog at Chara Gladey's Blog

Join my newsletter for the exclusive Chara Gladey's Newsletter

Sign up for Free Stories from Xplicit Press AuthorsCandra Aubrey's Blog

Xplicit Press Author Updates

Like Xplicit Press on Facebook

Follow Xplicit Press on Twitter

Readers: I want to expand a few of the stories to see where the characters can be explored further. If there are any of the stories that you would like to read more about again, I'd love to hear from you!

Keep In Touch
Chara Gladey
info@charagladey.com